Boris the Cat

Erwin Moser was born in Vienna, Austria in 1954 and
grew up in a village on Lake Neusiedl. He trained
as a typesetter, and in 1980 began to create and
illustrate his enchanting tales. For more than
thirty years he published numerous children's picture
books, for which he received many awards and was
shortlisted for the German Youth Literature Prize.
His books, imaginatively written and illustrated,
are remarkable for their warmheartedness and have
earned their place in the canon of German-language
literature for children and young adults. In 2014 the
Erwin Moser Museum was opened in his home
village of Gols. Erwin Moser died in 2017.

Erwin Moser

Boris the Cat

The Little Cat with Big Ideas

Translated by Alistair Beaton

Contents

Boris the cat floated down the river in a little barrel.
Where had he come from? Nobody knew.

A storm was coming. At a bend of the river he got out.
An owl was watching him.

Boris Arrives

It started to rain. The owl was curious and followed Boris.

Boris stood under a tree to get out of the rain. "I know an empty house that you might like," said the owl.

The owl led Boris to a little house. The rain got worse.

Inside the house it was nice and dry. The first thing Boris did was try out the bed. "I like this house. I think I'll stay here for a while," he said.

Boris watched some storks trying to build their nest in an old dead tree. "Looks like hard work," thought Boris.

After a while Boris got bored and walked up a hill. At the top he found an old automobile tire.

The Storks

Boris liked to be comfortable. He set up the tire and settled down inside it for a snooze. A little mouse appeared and started playing around with the tire.

The mouse pushed the tire down the hill. A rude awakening for Boris! He didn't know what was happening to him.

The tire rolled down toward the pond and bounced into the tree where the storks were building their nest.

Nobody was hurt. In fact, the tire delighted the storks. It's going to make it much easier for them to build their nest!

One morning Boris saw a baby carriage floating down the river. "Oh, how awful!" thought Boris. "I've got to save the baby."

Boris tried to hook the carriage with a stick, but the stick wasn't long enough.

The Baby Carriage

Instead he went farther downstream and tried
to catch the carriage from a bridge.
He missed again.

There was nothing else to do: he had to jump
in the water.

He swam after the baby carriage as fast as he could.
At last he reached it and pushed it to the bank
of the river.

But the "baby" he saved was actually a frog who
was using the carriage as a boat!

Today the wildcat was coming to visit Boris. He decided to welcome her with a gigantic bunch of flowers.

Boris headed home, pulling a cart full of flowers behind him. He picked so many he could easily make *three* bunches of flowers!

The Bouquet of Flowers

Boris didn't notice that as he went along the flowers were gradually falling off.

When he reached home he was shocked to see what had happened.

Oh, no! Here comes the wildcat!

"Boris!" she exclaimed. "You covered the path with flowers, just for me. What a lovely thing to do!"

"You're just in time!" Holly the Hedgehog said to Boris. "My new invention is ready. I've fed this daisy with my super-fertilizer!"

"And now watch. First I cut the daisy. Then I screw it into this fantastic machine. And then I start the engine. Come on, Boris, climb aboard!"

The Helicopter

The engine roared, the daisy began to revolve like the rotor blades of a helicopter, and the box lifted up.

Everything was going like clockwork! Holly piloted the wooden helicopter across the pond until suddenly the flower started losing its petals.

More and more petals fell off. The engine howled and the helicopter crashed into the pond. *Splash!*

But things were not as bad as they looked. The wooden box was watertight, and just to be on the safe side Holly brought a sail with her.

Boris was painting his front door. He was expecting a visit from Bruno the Bear.

He kept chasing away the pesky birds that were eating up all his grass seeds.

The Scarecrow

As Boris stared at the useless scarecrow, he suddenly had an interesting idea.

The cat painted his face blue. He reckoned this would really scare those birds away!

They started coming back. Boris waited until they all landed.

Then as loudly as he could, he shouted, "GO AWAY!" Oh dear, he scared off Bruno as well, just as Bruno was arriving!

It was windy and rainy. But Boris still wanted to go for a walk. He opened his red umbrella.

Out in the fields the wind was even stronger. That's when Boris met a little seagull.

The Umbrella

"Poor little seagull," said Boris. "Too scared to fly in this weather? Come here. Let me warm you up."

Just as he crossed a bridge over the river, a gust of wind caught Boris's umbrella and turned it inside out.

On the other bank of the river Boris found a tree with a big empty bird's nest in it.

Boris got into the nest along with the seagull. He hung his umbrella from a branch above them. The little seagull was happy again.

Boris and Holly the Hedgehog had an early start.
Holly was planning to go into the mountains and
spend the night in a tent.

Boris went along to help Holly.
Up at this height there was a strong wind blowing.

The Tent

When they tried to put the tent up,
the wind caught the cloth and inflated it.

Boris and Holly tried hard to hold the tent down,
but suddenly the wind lifted them both high
in the air.

The wind blew the two friends back to where they
started. Boris and Holly drifted to earth as if they
had a parachute.

They landed right in front of Holly's house.
"That was great!" said Boris. "Come on,
let's do it again right now!"

One day Sophie the Squirrel gave Boris
a goldfish as a present.

Boris watched the goldfish for a while.
"He's lovely," he thought.
"But he has so little space to swim."

The Goldfish

Boris soon decided to take the goldfish down to the river. "Let's see how he reacts when he sees so much water!"

"Look at the big river," said Boris. "Do you like it?"

Suddenly the overhanging bank gave way and Boris fell into the river—along with the goldfish bowl!

The goldfish was free and swam around merrily in the river. Alex the Frog saw what happened. "Don't worry, Boris," he said. "I'll look after him."

Holly the Hedgehog went to town and bought a new worktable. Boris helped her carry it back home.
"Hurry up, Boris. There's a storm coming," said Holly.

Out in the middle of a field, they were hit by a fierce wind. Boris and Holly couldn't go on. They tipped over the table and used it as a windbreak.

The Table

Next the rain came pelting down. Holly and Boris hurriedly turned the table the right way up and crawled underneath. That way they stayed dry!

When the rain eased up a little, they continued on their way. Holly and Boris were now holding the table above their heads. But that soon became too tiring.

It finally stopped raining. At the top of a slope, Boris and Holly turned over the table, climbed on, and slid down the hill over the wet grass.

Holly and Boris were pleased with the new table. They celebrated by having a snack on it. A very big snack!

Alex the Frog popped up and said, "The frogs are putting on a concert tonight, and you're invited, Boris! It will be on the old tree trunk down by the reed beds."

As it got dark, Boris put on a bow tie, got out his top hat, and headed for the concert.

The Concert

Boris was the only member of the audience.
The six frogs sang their hearts out.

Boris was so enchanted by the music
that he shut his eyes and sang along.

The frogs didn't like the sound of a cat singing.
They clapped their hands over their ears and
jumped off the tree trunk as fast as they could.

When Boris opened his eyes again, all the frogs
were gone. "Weird," thought Boris.
"That was a very short concert."

Boris borrowed a pile of books from Biff the Badger's underground library. There were so many books he couldn't carry them all.

The badger had a strange suggestion for how Boris could get the books back home. He found an old rubber dinghy in his storeroom and pumped it up.

The Emergency Exit

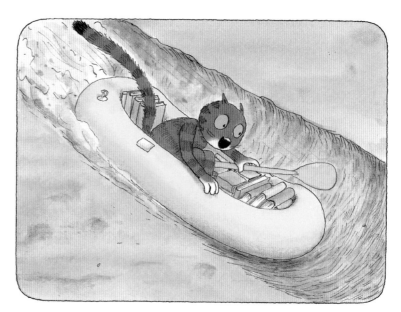

Then the two of them carried the dinghy and the books down to a cave. "This is my emergency exit," said Biff. "Don't be scared, Boris. Just jump in the boat!"

Biff the Badger gave the boat a push into a steep tunnel. Boris went whooshing down through the badger's emergency exit.

Suddenly there was light ahead and the dinghy shot out into the open. The emergency exit led straight into the river! With a loud splash Boris landed in the water.

But all was well. Boris and the books were both dry. Feeing contented, Boris paddled homeward with his treasure trove of books.

Boris wanted to have a bath, but the bathtub sprang a leak. The owl knew someone who could repair it.

Boris picked up the heavy bathtub, and the owl led him to the workshop of Holly the Hedgehog.

The Traveling Bathtub

Holly could repair anything.
"Come back tomorrow,' she said, "and this bathtub
will be as good as new."

It was after midnight, and the lights were still
on in Holly's workshop. Inside there was a lot of
hammering and welding going on. Very odd . . .

When Boris and the owl returned to the workshop,
they could hardly believe their eyes. Holly had
turned the bathtub into an automobile!

Holly's inventions could be a bit crazy. Boris didn't
mind at all. The traveling bathtub was fantastic!
And anyway, cats don't like getting wet, do they?

Boris was in the mountains trying out his new traveling bathtub. He was very pleased. The engine was powerful enough to take him up the steepest slopes.

He ran into Bruno the Bear. Bruno was going on vacation; but he had slept in, and now he was afraid that he'd miss his train.

The Crash

No problem! Boris invited the bear to climb aboard
and zoomed off at high speed down a mountain road.

But Boris was going much too fast.
He couldn't make the bend in the road.
Bruno covered his eyes.

They went hurtling toward the ground!
At that very moment, Bruno's train came out
of the tunnel.

They landed on the second railroad car,
which was loaded with straw. Weren't they lucky!
And Bruno caught his train after all.

It was a warm summer's day.
Boris the Cat was going to try out his
new hammock and read his book.

The distance between the two small trees
in the backyard was perfect for a hammock.

The Hammock

Well, the distance was right, but the trees
were too thin. Boris thought hard.

He went into the house and brought out
a big pumpkin. But would his plan work?

Boris put the pumpkin into the hammock.
The trees bent together again. Boris got a ladder,
climbed up . . .

. . . and lay down in the soft bed of leaves
provided by the two trees. It's not every day
you see a mattress made of leaves!

For weeks Holly the Hedgehog had been building a boat. She sent Boris into the next village to buy a can of black paint.

Boris headed back with the can of paint in his hands. Holly was in a hurry for the paint, so Boris decided to take a shortcut through a field of marigolds.

The Can of Paint

Boris ran through the marigolds, making all the pollen whirl up until he was yellow from top to toe.

At the end of the marigold field Boris didn't notice a puddle of rainwater. He stumbled and slipped on the muddy ground.

Boris landed in the puddle and the can flew out of his hands. As the lid came off, a fountain of black paint sprayed out.

Soon after, Boris reached Holly's workshop. "Help!" she screamed. "Boris, is that really you? I thought you were a tiger!"

Boris wanted to give Bruno the Bear the biggest strawberry in his garden as a present. But it was a long way to Bruno's house and the strawberry was very heavy.

Boris took a break. Then along came the polecat that wanted to swap his beautiful hat for the strawberry. Boris agreed.

The Swap

But the hat would be far too small for Bruno!
So Boris swapped it for the water rat's
swimming mask.

Then Boris remembered that Bruno the Bear
never goes swimming. So he found Alex the Frog
and swapped the swimming mask for a water lily.

Boris gave the water lily to the wildcat,
and in return the wildcat gave Boris a jar of honey.
Fantastic! Just the right present for Bruno!

When Boris got to Bruno's house,
Bruno was in the middle of filling dozens
of jars with . . . honey!

Bruno the Bear was balancing on a ball. He was practicing a circus trick. "Can I try that?" asked Boris.

"Yes, but be careful," said Bruno. The warning came too late. Boris bounced up and down on the ball and was thrown off.

The Ball

Boris went tumbling down the steep mountain slope . . .

. . . and splashed straight into the river.

Boris was shocked. He grabbed ahold of the ball and swam down the river until he got to his house.

Not long after, Bruno arrived. "Hey, Boris, what you did back there really was something else!" he said. "Here's a bar of chocolate to make you feel better."

One lovely summer morning Boris left his house.
He carefully locked the door.
He was carrying a bulging duffel bag on his back.

Bruno the Bear happened to be on his morning walk.
"Hello, Boris, where are you going?" he asked.
"Holly built a boat. We're going on a voyage!" said Boris.

The Boat

Bruno decided to go with him. Bruno knew all about
Holly's inventions. They often didn't work! But when the
bear saw the beautiful steamboat, he was very impressed.

The boat was on a frame with four wheels.
That made it easy to move.
Together they transported the boat to the river.

Thanks to the strength of the bear, the boat was soon
in the water. Holly the Hedgehog got the steam engine
going, and the white-painted boat set off.

"So long, Bruno!" shouted Boris. Bruno shouted back,
"Safe journey! Send me a postcard!" Bruno watched
till the boat disappeared around a bend in the river.

Boris was fishing in the river.
But instead of catching fish he caught junk.
He already caught a pot, an umbrella . . .

. . . a straw hat, a glass bottle, and a boot.
Hold on! There was something heavy on the line.

The Fishing Rod

Boris reeled in the fish he thought he caught.
It was so heavy it bent the fishing rod! But it wasn't
a fish. This time it was an old chair.

Boris had an idea. He wrote a note:
Does anyone live down there? He stuffed it into
the bottle. Then he threw the bottle into the river.

Guess what? Someone did live down there!
It was Alex the Frog. His home was an old shipwreck.
Alex read the message in the bottle.

Alex popped up. "Hi, Boris!" he said.
Thanks for helping me get rid of all that junk
I had in my house!"

Boris meets Holly behind her workshop.
"It's great you're here, Boris," said Holly,
"I'm in the middle of an experiment."

"You see, I've invented a super-fertilizer:
I pour three drops of it onto this pansy.
Now watch what happens!"

The Pansy

Boris watched, astonished.
Within seconds the pansy doubled in size.
And it kept growing!

"It works, it works!" shouted Holly the Hedgehog.
By now the flower was as big as both of them.

It still wouldn't stop growing!
Boris and Holly found it a bit scary.

It looked as if the pansy was making an
angry face at them. Boris and Holly ran away
as fast as they could.

Boris was climbing a high mountain.
Biff the Badger asked him to paint
a mountain landscape.

As he got near the summit, Boris was hit by
a sudden rockslide. But the canvas kept him safe.

The Picture

Just as he got to the summit, it started to rain.
Boris held up the canvas as a roof over his head!

It was clear there was not going to be any painting
done today. The cat set off back down the mountain.
Now the canvas was his sled!

Boris whizzed down the mountain across the loose
stones—straight into the badger's den!

"Oh, Boris, it's you!" exclaimed Biff the Badger.
"Finished the painting already? That was fast!"

Boris was painting his house.
But he didn't have a ladder and wondered
how he was going to reach the high parts.

Suddenly someone tapped him on the shoulder.
Frightened, Boris jumped, turned around,
and saw an elephant standing in front of him!

The Elephant

"Where on earth did you come from?" asked Boris.
"Aha, you probably ran away from the circus!"

Boris had an idea. That elephant turned up
just in time! With his help Boris was able to finish
painting the house.

They both had fun doing the work.
That evening Boris rode the elephant back
to the circus tent.

They arrived just in time for the evening performance.
The two clowns were astonished to see
the new performers!

Holly the Hedgehog repaired an old bike and painted it red. She gave it to Boris.

Boris was thrilled. It had been ages since he rode a bike. He decided to try it out immediately.

The Bicycle

Boris cycled to the riverbank.
It was hard going uphill.
Boris found it difficult to keep his balance.

But going downhill was fantastic!
Boris hurtled down the embankment toward the river.
But . . . where were the brakes?

Boris couldn't stop. The branch of a tree saved him
from having an unexpected bath!

The red bike disappeared into the river.
Now Alex the Frog had it.

Holly the Hedgehog built a plane.
Boris helped her push it to the top of a hill.
It was a glider.

The two of them climbed aboard and let it
roll down the hill. Would it fly?
Yes, the glider took off brilliantly!

The Airplane

What was that?! There was a loud crack
as one of the wings broke off and spun toward
the ground.

No more hope of flying! Holly and Boris crash-landed.
Luckily for them, the water broke their fall.

A big pelican heard the splash and came
out of the reeds.
"I'll show you how to fly," he told them.

Holly sat on the pelican's back while Boris climbed
into the pouch of the pelican's beak.
Yes, the pelican was the perfect airplane!

Boris found a wooden crate.
He planned to paddle over to the little island
in the river.

It soon became clear that the crate
wasn't watertight. The river came gurgling in.

The Turtle

Boris felt sorry for himself as he climbed up the riverbank. He saw a big stone where he could sit down and let his fur dry.

Boris fell asleep. The stone moved. It was actually a turtle!

The turtle crawled to the water's edge and swam to the island. Did he know what Boris was hoping to do?

When Boris woke up, the turtle was asleep again. Boris looked around and was very confused.

Boris was hurrying to get home. It was late,
it was raining, and there was a storm coming up.
From inside a bush, four gleaming eyes watched him.

As Boris reached home, the four eyes
appeared again. They scared him.
He quickly closed the front door behind him.

The Owls

Boris got into bed. There was a scratching noise
at the window. Four yellow eyes shone in the darkness.
Who on earth could that be?

Boris plucked up all his courage, lit a candle,
and opened the window. He discovered two little owls
looking for shelter from the storm.

The excited young owls explained to Boris
that it was so hard to fly in the storm that they
couldn't find their way home.

Boris knew where the owls lived.
He promised to take them home first thing in
the morning. Reassured, all three of them fell asleep.

Boris cleared out his attic.
His cart was full of things he didn't need anymore.

But maybe somebody else could use them?
The old coat stand got a great response
from the Owl family.

Gifts from the Attic

The big salad bowl would make an
elegant bathtub for the field mice!
(Do mice even take baths?)

Sophie the Squirrel found the butterfly net perfect.
In the autumn she'd use it to collect nuts
from the trees.

Alex the Frog immediately realized that the
drawer with the cooking spoon was really a boat
with a paddle!

And the armchair? Boris kept that.
He took it to the top of a hill, sat down,
and enjoyed the beautiful sunset.

One evening Boris found a big red book
lying in a garbage dump.
It looked like an exciting cat story!

Boris decided to carry the big red book home.
It was really heavy.

The Book

The cat had to take a break.
That's when he met a sad little mouse who
didn't know where she would sleep that night.

A storm blew the roof off of her house.
The mouse was in a panic. Nearly in tears,
she led Boris to her ruined home.

"What am I going to do?" she asked.
"If it starts to rain, I'll be soaked through!"
Boris had a brilliant idea.

He opened the big red book in the middle and
laid it across the little house.
The new roof fit perfectly! The mouse danced with joy.

One day two broom-makers came to Boris's house.
"Maybe you need a new broom, Mr. Cat?"
one of them asked. "Yes, I do!" said Boris.

"These brooms are the best; they'll last forever," said the
other one. Boris fetched some money. Because the two of
them looked so poor, he bought every broom they had.

The Brooms

"Now, what am I going to do with all these brooms?" wondered Boris. And then he had an idea.

He leaned one broom against the wall of the house and carried the others to a hole in the garden fence.

Boris had been meaning to mend the fence for ages. Now he used the brooms to do it.

Finally he trimmed them all like a hedge. "Who knows? Maybe soon they'll flower," he thought.

"Look, Boris," said Holly the Hedgehog.
"This time I've built something that's guaranteed to work, a hot air balloon! Come on, climb aboard!"

Holly let go of the anchor ropes, and the balloon rose slowly and elegantly in the air.
It was the perfect day for a balloon trip.

The Balloon

Soon they were floating over the mountains and
above the home of Bruno the Bear.
Bruno saw the balloon and waved to them.

A big old crow also spotted the balloon.
The shape of the balloon reminded him of a sausage,
so he pecked at it to have a taste.

The air whistled out through the hole the crow made,
and the balloon began to fall. Holly and Boris were
terrified. Even the crow was terrified!

The crow shrieked loudly and flew off.
The punctured balloon crashed into a bush.
Luckily, Holly and Boris were not hurt.

Boris was helping the Hare family bring
in the apple harvest.
They'd been picking apples all day long.

The Hares thanked Boris and gave him
a crate of apples to take home.
It was very heavy.

The Apple Harvest

The farther he went, the heavier the crate seemed to become. He tried carrying it on his back.

Phew! Boris was worn out.
He took a break and then heard the sound of a truck approaching.

It was a balloon-seller. Boris traded a few apples for some balloons.

Boris tied the balloons to his crate of apples.
Now it was really easy to take them home!

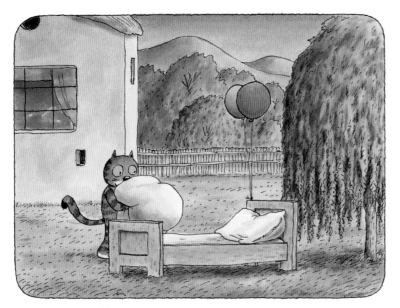

It was a really warm autumn evening.
Boris had set up his bed beside the willow tree
in the garden.

He liked the idea of sleeping outside that night.
He tied his two favorite balloons to the bed.

The Dream

Boris dreamed that the two balloons carried him over the sea to a castle on an island.

But suddenly it began to storm.
The balloons burst. As he fell into the water, something grabbed on to his leg.

A big scary octopus held him tight and pulled him down to the seabed!

Boris woke up. It was raining.
He'd fallen out of bed, and the willow branches felt like tentacles!

One night Boris woke up suddenly.
He heard a noise somewhere in the house.
There it was again! It was coming from the kitchen.

Boris snuck downstairs to the kitchen and
switched on the light. A little mouse was eating
Boris's cheese! The mouse was terrified.

The Mushrooms

"Don't be scared," said Boris.
"I've got plenty of cheese.
You can have the whole piece."

Two days later Boris was going through
the woods looking for mushrooms.
Sadly, he couldn't find a single one.

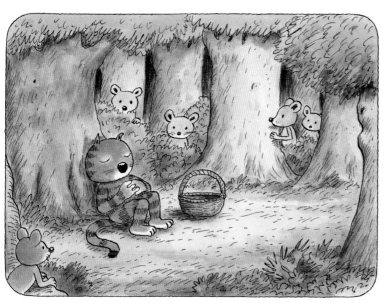

Feeling tired, Boris found a clearing in the woods and
had a snooze. There was a rustling in the bushes.
Five little mice stared at the sleeping cat.

An hour later Boris woke up and found a mountain
of mushrooms beside him. What do you think?
Could they have been from the little mice?

The leaves were changing color and
the nights turned chilly. Boris went into the forest
to cut some wood for the stove.

He ran into Sophie the Squirrel.
"Hello, Boris," she said.
"How do you like my new tree house?"

The Kayak

"Very cozy," said Boris. "But I thought you lived beside the river."
"I used to," said Sophie. "But a storm blew down my tree."

The squirrel led Boris to the fallen tree. When he saw the squirrel's two entrance holes in the trunk, Boris had an idea.

Boris swung his ax and chopped off the roots and the branches. Sophie was curious.
"What's the plan?" she asked.

A few hours later Boris had finished. He turned the old tree house into a kayak!

Boris was about to water his pumpkin when Holly the Hedgehog turned up and cried out, "Boris, wait! Let me try out my super-fertilizer on the pumpkin."

The hedgehog poured a few drops of the strange liquid on to the pumpkin. Boris had seen Holly's fertilizer before. He knew what was about to happen.

The Pumpkin

Just as he thought, within a minute the pumpkin had doubled in size. "What am I supposed to do with a pumpkin that big?" asked Boris.

The pumpkin kept growing until it was five or six times the size it once was! Holly said, "Boris, I have an idea. Get two kitchen knives."

Boris and Holly cut three holes in the giant pumpkin and hollowed it out.

Inside the hollow pumpkin they set up a table and two chairs. Now they had their own summerhouse!

Boris was out on a quest with Biff the Badger.
Biff was sure his divining rod would help him track
down buried treasure.

Suddenly the rod started pointing to the ground.
"There's treasure down there!" said Biff excitedly.
"I'm sure of it. Start digging, Boris!"

The Dowsing Rod

The two of them worked hard to dig a hole in the ground.
"How deep do we have to go?" asked Boris. "Not much
farther now," said Biff. "I can feel something already!"

But what Biff felt was the earth moving!
They dug so deep that they found themselves falling
into a hamster's den.

Boris and Biff weren't hurt by the fall,
but now they had to listen to the angry complaints
of the hamster.

"You're expecting to find buried treasure here?"
asked the hamster. "Are you nuts?"

Boris the Cat found an old faux-fur coat in his attic.
He liked the look of it.

It was getting colder with every day that passed,
so a warm coat would be useful.
Boris went for a walk to try it out.

The Faux-Fur Coat

The coat was very heavy and much too warm for Boris.
He saw a man in a field and went over to him.

It wasn't a man at all. It was a scarecrow.
A little mouse lived inside the scarecrow.
She told Boris that she was cold at night.

"I don't really need this coat at all," said Boris.
"I already have a nice thick fur of my own."
He put the coat on the scarecrow.

Then he buttoned up the coat.
"Ah, you've made it all lovely and warm in here!"
squeaked the mouse. "Now winter can come, no problem!"

"Look, Boris, I invented a snow-making machine!"
said Holly the Hedgehog.

"Watch. Here comes the first snow."
Holly pulled down a lever. Boris was amazed.
"It really works!" he said.

The Snow-Making Machine

The machine hummed and spat out
more and more snow up in the air.
"Fantastic! It's snowing, it's snowing!" shouted Boris.

The blizzard got thicker and thicker—
Boris and Holly could hardly see a thing.
When it got even worse, Boris and Holly ran away.

When they came back a half hour later,
Holly's house was all snowed in.
The scary snow machine had finally stopped.

Then it started snowing for real!
"You should have invented a snow-
melting machine instead," said Boris.

Harold and Frieda, the wild boars, really liked their food. So they asked Boris to bake a cake for them. They knew he made very good cakes.

Boris carried the cake across the meadows to where the wild boars lived. But there was a storm coming, complete with thunder and lightning!

The Puffball

The rain poured down.
Boris ran as fast as he could so the cake
wouldn't get wet.

Suddenly he stumbled over something, and his
beautiful cake went "*splat!*" against the trunk of a tree.
"Oh, Boris, why didn't you look where you were going?"

Then Boris realized he had stumbled over a giant
mushroom—a puffball!
Puffballs are a delicacy and hard to find.

Instead of bringing the cake, Boris brought
the puffball. Harold and Frieda were thrilled
and invited Boris to have dinner with them.

Holly the Hedgehog and Boris agreed to climb a mountain. But Boris had been waiting two hours for her to arrive.

After waiting for another hour with no sign of the hedgehog, Boris decided to climb the mountain on his own.

The Eagle

Suddenly Boris saw his friend waving to him from
the top of the opposite mountain.
Boris climbed the wrong mountain!

Farther on Boris came across an eagle's nest.
Boris offered to give the eagle a whole salami
if the eagle would help him.

The eagle agreed. He grabbed Boris's backpack
in his talons and flew Boris over to the other mountain.

At the top of the mountain the eagle let go of Boris.
"Hi there, Holly!" said Boris, landing gracefully
on all four paws.

While out hiking, Boris discovered a mountain kitten swinging from the branch of a tree. Boris thought the kitten was in danger and lifted her down.

"You could have fallen into the ravine!" said a worried Boris. "Where do you live?"
The kitten pointed to the other side of the ravine.

The Kitten

There was a tree trunk lying across the ravine. It was the only way to get to the other side. Trembling with fear, Boris stepped onto the bridge. He felt dizzy.

And then it happened. Boris slipped and fell. Quick as lightning the kitten leaped out of his arms.

Boris managed to cling to the tree trunk. The mountain kitten, who was obviously very smart and not afraid of heights, called for her mom.

Together they got Boris onto his feet and led him safely across the bridge.

One dark and rainy day Boris went for a walk.
He wanted to try out his new coat, his new boots,
and his new umbrella.

A sudden gust of wind tore the umbrella
from his hands. The umbrella disappeared behind a
thornbush.

The Bat

Boris wanted to get his umbrella back.
But his coat got caught in the branches of the
thornbush, and he had to take it off.

There was a swamp behind the thornbush.
This is where the bat lived.
She saw that Boris was in trouble.

Next Boris lost his boots in the swamp.
The bat pulled the cat onto dry land.

It was warm and cozy in the bat's cave.
"Thanks," said Boris. "I've always been afraid of you,
but now I know you're really friendly!"

When Boris woke up, he had an idea for a fairy tale.
He spent the whole morning writing it.

The fairy tale was finished. Boris hurried to the house of his inventor friend, Holly the Hedgehog. Boris wanted to read the fairy tale to her.

The Fairy Tale

But Holly was busy working on a new invention and
didn't want to be disturbed. "Come back tomorrow,
Boris," she said.

Boris walked back home through the wood,
reading his fairy tale out loud to himself.
Two shy little mice were watching him.

Boris sat down on a tree stump in a clearing and
continued reading his fairy tale out loud.
More and more mice appeared and listened to him.

Soon the clearing was full of mice.
Boris had to start again at the beginning.
But he was more than happy to do that!

Boris called Biff the Badger in order to borrow some books. Biff told him about his secret treasure trove.

Boris asked to see the treasure trove.
The badger lit a lamp. "Follow me," he said.

The Treasure Trove

They went through a long tunnel in the mountain, then across a rope bridge and into a cave.

They went down a staircase and came to an underground lake.
"Just a short boat trip now," said Biff.

Boris found it a bit scary. The badger paddled the boat across the lake until they came to the entrance to the treasure trove.

The treasure trove was a gigantic library!
"Choose any book you like," said Biff.
Boris was speechless.

One warm summer's day Boris and
Holly the Hedgehog went hiking in the mountains.

Hiking makes you hungry.
At lunchtime they found a nice spot and
unpacked all their food.

The Picnic

Boris and Holly ate much too much.
They flopped down in the shade and
had a little snooze.

Once they recovered from their lunch they decided
to head home. There was a flash of lightning!
A storm was approaching.

They came to the owl's tree house.
"You two look very tired," said the owl.
"Would you like to try out my tree house bed?"

Boris and Holly leaped at the idea.
It started to rain. The owl wished he
hadn't invited them in.

Boris went to an antique shop in town and bought himself an old grandfather clock.

Boris took it back home in his handcart.
He wondered where in the house it should go.

The Clock

He stopped for a rest and took a closer look
at the clock. That's when he found a frightened mouse—
inside the clock!

The little mouse was too scared to come out.
She was a town mouse and didn't know anyone who
lived in the country.

Boris had a solution. He stood the clock up
against a tree in the woods.
He'd come back and get it tomorrow.

The minute Boris left, all the country mice
came out and invited the town mouse to come
and live with them.

Boris didn't know his date of birth.
One evening Sophie the Squirrel sent him
to see the short-eared owl.

"Why does the short-eared owl want to see me?"
wondered Boris. (Everybody knew the owl
was a fortune-teller.)

The Birthday

"Good to see you, Boris," said the owl.
"My crystal ball has revealed one of your secrets!"

"Listen, Boris. You came into the world exactly seven years ago, and today you've got a surprise coming."

Boris didn't know whether to believe the owl.
When he got back home, he found his house all lit up.

Nearly all his friends were waiting for him.
They brought presents, and they all shouted,
"Happy birthday, Boris!"

It was bitterly cold and the pond had frozen over.
Boris got out his ice skates.

Boris glided elegantly across the fresh ice.
Holly the Hedgehog's house was nearby.
Boris decided to pay her a visit.

The Armchair

Holly was sitting in an armchair at the edge of the frozen pond. "I'd like to go skating too," she said. "But I've sprained my ankle."

Boris had an idea. He took his skates off and attached them to the front legs of the chair.

Then he attached Holly's skates to the back legs of the chair. The hedgehog looked on in amazement.

But would it work? Boris pushed the armchair across the ice. Holly gave directions. Yes, it worked. It was fantastic!

The forest ranger gave Boris permission
to choose a Christmas tree.

"This one's perfect," thought the cat,
and chopped down a big fir tree.

The Christmas Tree

Oh, Boris, that was a big mistake!
The tree was much too heavy to carry home!

Boris cut the tree in two.
The crow couldn't figure it out.

It was still too heavy!
He'd have to chop a bit more off.

Boris ended up going home with just a tiny treetop.
The forest ranger was not going to be happy!

It would soon be Christmas.
Boris the Cat spent the whole day in
the kitchen baking Christmas cookies.

His Christmas cookies were perfect!
Boris made a quick decision. He filled his backpack
with cookies and set off into the mountains.

The Christmas Cookies

Boris planned to visit his friend Bruno the Bear and give him a present of Christmas cookies. That would make Bruno happy! But Boris got caught in a snowstorm.

For hours on end Boris wandered around in the snowstorm, completely lost. He couldn't find the bear's house. He was so hungry and desperate that he ate all the cookies himself!

Suddenly a wall of snow collapsed and Bruno looked out. His house was completely snowed in.

Indoors it was all warm and snug. Bruno had been baking too. But Boris couldn't face the thought of any more Christmas cookies!

It was freezing cold. The crows in the tree gazed
longingly at Boris's warm and cozy little house.

Boris had a slight cold.
He was sitting up in bed reading a book.

The Crows

After a while Boris got bored.
He looked out of the window. The minute they saw him,
the crows flew over to the house.

"Those poor birds," thought Boris.
"They must be hungry."
He gathered some seeds and fed the crows.

When the crows had enough to eat,
Boris invited them into his room.
They didn't need to be asked twice!

Now the crows were warm too, and Boris had company.
He read them a story from his book.

One day Boris went to visit Holly and discovered that she had just come up with a new invention.

It was a tractor on skis, powered by steam. Holly invited Boris to have a test drive and explained how the tractor worked.

The Steam-Tractor Sled

"This machine can overcome any obstacle," said Holly proudly. "It can even go up steep hills."

"And going down you never lose control. Just watch: it can even travel on ice."

But the tractor was too heavy and the ice broke! The hot boiler hissed loudly as it hit the water.

A huge cloud of steam rose up in the air. Holly was embarrassed. "Hmm," she said. "Maybe it's not quite right for traveling on ice!"

Boris was going to a costume party
dressed as Puss in Boots.
He looked at himself in the mirror.

He set off. He had to hurry. He wanted to
pick up Holly the Hedgehog on the way.
He wondered what costume she would be wearing.

The Burglar

Boris suddenly stopped.
He realized he left the lights on and
hadn't locked the front door.

As Boris got back home he saw
a figure in black at the door.
"A burglar!" he thought.

With sword drawn, Boris descended on
the masked figure. "Stop! Get away from that door!"
The burglar spun around in shock.

"Boris, it's me! Holly the Hedgehog!" cried the
figure in black, and took off her mask and hat.
"I was coming to pick you up on the way to the party!"

It was a beautiful winter's day, and
Boris wanted to go ski jumping.

Boris skied fearlessly down the steep slope.

The Ski Jumper

Then he came to the ramp at the edge of a cliff.

Boris took off and flew into space.
His posture was perfect.

Boris folded his arms but kept floating higher and
higher. What was going on?!

Ah, so that's it! Well, have a good flight,
the three of you!

Boris had been visiting his friend Bruno the Bear.
Just as Boris was leaving, Bruno gave him a huge
Christmas present.

The bear told Boris not to open it until he got home.
The package was quite bulky.

The Postage Stamps

After walking for a while, it became too heavy to carry.
What could be in it?

Boris opened the package.
It was a box full of stamps.
Suddenly there was a gust of wind . . .

. . . that blew the stamps up in the air.
Now it was snowing stamps! What a disaster!

"Never mind," thought Boris.
"Collecting stamps is boring anyway.
But the box makes a good sled!"

The pond had just frozen overnight.
Boris and Holly were about to go skating.
Alex the Frog was already showing off on the ice.

Suddenly the ice cracked—and Alex fell through.
The ice wasn't thick enough yet for skating.

Going Skating

Holly and Boris wanted to help the frog, but Alex said he was fine. He was a frog; he had no problems with water. In no time at all he clambered back onto the ice.

Alex continued skating merrily. Boris was afraid to go onto the ice. But Holly had an idea.
"Follow me, Boris," she said.

They disappeared into Holly's workshop, and after a while both came out wearing very strange outfits.

Holly found diving suits in her amazing inventor's workshop. Now the two friends were safe as safe could be.

Boris was looking for the badger's den.
There had been a lot of snow over the last few days,
and the forest looked quite different.

Boris couldn't find the badger's den.
He lit a campfire to keep himself warm.
Suddenly a wildcat appeared.

Lost

She sat down beside Boris at the fire.
The wildcat was a newcomer to the forest.
She didn't know where the badger lived.

The two of them got sleepy and dozed off.
The fire slowly burned out, and it began
to snow again.

They awoke to find the badger standing in front
of them, holding up a lamp. "What are you doing here?"
he said. "Come into my nice warm den."

It was really cozy in the badger's den.
Boris and the wildcat were given hot tea
and allowed to stay the night.

Boris rolled a big snowball. He planned
to build a snowman on the top of the hill
so that everyone could see it from miles around.

Boris got careless. The snowball slipped
away from him and rolled down the steep slope.

The Giant Snowball

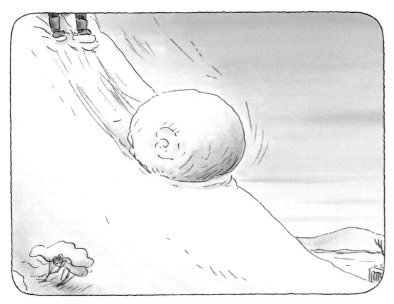

Boris leaped after it, but it was too late.
The snowball just went faster and faster and
got bigger and bigger.

Anna the Mouse lived at the foot of the hill.
The giant snowball flattened the fence around her
house and came to rest against a tree.

Anna looked out in surprise. Boris came rushing
down the hill. "Oh, I'm so sorry, Anna!
Please don't be angry!" he said.

Boris had an idea. He and Anna gave
the giant snowball a jolly snowman's face!

It was the twenty-fifth of December. Christmas Day!
Boris went through the woods looking for a suitable
Christmas tree.

He came to the tree house of Lisa the Dormouse.
"The children and I have colds," said Lisa.
"Better stay back, Boris, so you don't catch it!"

The Christmas Surprise

Boris chopped down a Christmas tree and walked back home. "That poor Dormouse family," he thought. "I'm going to give them a nice surprise."

Boris wrapped up a bundle of toys and cookies, and filled a bag with Christmas tree decorations. Then he went out, carrying a stepladder over his shoulder.

The shutters were closed over the window of Lisa's tree house. Boris quietly climbed the ladder and hung the Christmas tree decorations from the branches.

Then he knocked on the shutters and hid behind the tree. Moments later he hears excited shouts from Lisa and her children. . . .

Boris built a snowman beside the pond.
It looked a bit like Holly the Hedgehog.
"I'll have to show this to Holly right away!" he thought.

Boris found the hedgehog on the other side of the pond.
"Boris, look!" said Holly.
"A rocket sled driven by fireworks!"

The Rocket Sled

Holly got onto the sled. "I'm ready!" she said.
"Light the fuse, Boris. Watch out! Here I go!"

Boris just managed to jump out of the way
as two flames roared out of the rockets and
the sled zoomed off with Holly on it.

The speeding sled roared across the frozen pond.
Straight toward the snowman!

As Holly collided with the snowman
the fireworks exploded. But Holly was lucky.
The snowman provided a soft landing.

Holly the Hedgehog came hurtling down
the slope on skis. "Not so fast!" shouted Boris.
"Don't you want to try it?" asked Holly.

"I'm no good on skis," said Boris.
"Come on, I can see Bruno the Bear's house;
maybe we'll get coffee and cake."

The Sofa

But Holly had a better idea. "Do you have an old sofa that you don't need anymore?" she asked Bruno. The bear thought about it.

Holly was in luck. Bruno came out with an old two-seater sofa. "Excellent," said Holly. "Now all I need is a hammer and some nails."

Holly nailed her skis to the feet of the sofa. Bruno and Boris knew what she was up to.

Holly built a "sofa-sled" for herself and Boris. Now even Boris agrees that skiing is fun!

Boris and Holly the Hedgehog had been wandering around in the woods for hours. They were looking for the entrance to Biff the Badger's den.
Holly suddenly shouted, "Look, there it is!"

Holly shouted so loud that she started an avalanche! It thundered past them down the slope and blocked the entrance to the den.

The Avalanche

"Oh, poor Badger! I didn't mean it!" cried Holly the Hedgehog.
"Quick. We have to get him out of there," said Boris.
They began digging as fast as they could.

They heard a voice behind them.
"My friends! Stop digging. I'm safe and well!"
It was Biff the Badger.

"You know what? I have five other homes here in the
mountains. They're all connected," said the badger,
and led them to another entrance.

In the badger's cozy underground den
Boris and Holly were served tea.
Yes, visiting Biff the Badger was always a big event!

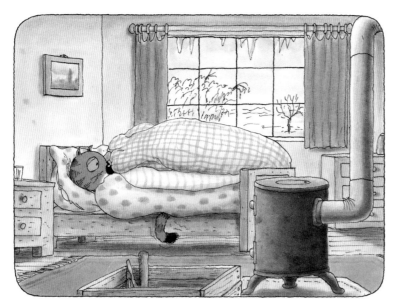

It was cold and frosty. What a bad time to run out of wood for the stove. Even with three blankets on the bed poor Boris was freezing.

"There's nothing else to do," thought Boris. "I'll have to go looking for firewood." He pulled on his boots and set off with his sled.

No Firewood

But even in the forest a blanket of snow covered everything. To get any firewood Boris would have to chop down a whole tree.

Then he came across a big nest. Katie the Dormouse looked out. "You must be frozen through," she said. "Come on in."

Boris managed to clamber into Katie's soft and comfortable nest. Ah, it was so cozy and warm in there!

Boris told the dormouse about his heating problems. She promptly invited him to spend the rest of the winter with her.

The Cat Secret

By Heinz Janisch

An afterword to Erwin Moser's marvelous stories

It's not only in the jungle that adventure awaits us, or in the desert, or out at sea. Adventure begins on our doorstep. Every path taken is an adventure. Whether I'm walking down the street, or strolling by the river, or running across a meadow—with each step everything is possible. Suddenly there's the glint of a stone among the grass, over there an old umbrella, here a snail sitting on the path, in the distance something creaking in the wind. Our adventure has already begun. The stone is a magic stone, the old umbrella will let you fly around the world, the snail speaks seven languages, and the creaking in the wind comes from a windmill that is only visible on Sundays. This is how storytelling begins.

In all walks of life there are people who are masters and mistresses of their craft, whether that be dressmaking, or baking bread, or playing football. For me, Erwin Moser is a master of storytelling. In words and pictures he tells adventure stories that could not be more delightful or more exciting. And why? Precisely because the adventure happens on your doorstep and because everything is possible. Whether it's little mice or big cats, little elephants or enchanted crows, the lovable characters in Erwin Moser's tales always find a way through, however sticky the situation. A pumpkin becomes a boat, a balloon becomes an airplane, a barrel becomes a sled…. The adventure begins with someone being fearless and inventive and trying out something new. And in doing so our little heroines and heroes find something else: they find friends who stick by them.

Erwin Moser was an important friend to me. I used to like visiting him in his workroom. There he'd be, sitting at his desk, his drawing pen in hand, in the midst of an adventure. And lying beside him on his desk—his cat. Purring. One day as I was busy stroking his cat I made a discovery. Was the purring not also coming from Erwin as he calmly wielded his pen? And suddenly I knew Erwin's cat secret: he had the soul of a cat! He loved the warmth of home as much as he loved the freedom of adventure.

With each of his stories, with each of his drawings, he sent us out into the world ready for whatever adventure might come our way. That's who we are: shrewd little cats, curious about the world and wanting to experience it. And with one elegant leap we throw ourselves into the next adventure.

Photograph Erwin Moser © 1985 by Hans Wetzelsdorfer

We thank the Austrian Federal Ministry for Art, Culture, Public Services,
and Sport for their financial support of this translation.

First published in the United States, Great Britain, Canada, Australia, and New Zealand in 2021 by
NorthSouth Books Inc., an imprint of NordSüd Verlag AG, CH-8050 Zürich, Switzerland.
Distributed in the United States by NorthSouth Books Inc., New York 10016.
Library of Congress Cataloging-in-Publication Data is available.
ISBN: 978-0-7358-4454-4
Printed in Livonia Print, Riga, Lettland